THE BALLAD OF

The

Pirate Queens

by

JANE YOLEN

ILLUSTRATED BY

DAVID SHANNON

Voyager Books
Harcourt, Inc.

Orlando   Austin   New York   San Diego   Toronto   London

For Bonnie, her book
— J. Y. and D. S.

Text copyright © 1995 by Jane Yolen
Illustrations copyright © 1995 by David Shannon

www.HarcourtBooks.com

First Voyager Books edition 1998
Voyager Books is a registered trademark of Harcourt, Inc.

The Library of Congress has cataloged the hardcover edition as follows:
Yolen, Jane.
The ballad of the pirate queens/written by Jane Yolen; illustrated by David Shannon.—1st ed.
p.   cm.
Summary: Two women who sailed with "Calico Jack" Rackham and his pirates in the early
1700s do their best to defend their ship while the men on board are busy drinking.
ISBN: 978-0-15-200710-2
ISBN: 978-0-15-201885-6 (pb)
1. Bonney, Anne, b. 1700—Juvenile fiction.   2. Reade, Mary, d. 1720? —Juvenile fiction.
[1. Bonney, Anne, b. 1700—Fiction.   2. Reade, Mary, d. 1720? —Fiction.
3. Pirates—Fiction.]   I. Shannon, David, 1959— ill.   II. Title
PZ7.Y78Bal   1995
[Fic]—dc20   94-7874

I K M O P N L J H

Printed in Singapore

The illustrations in this book were done in acrylic paint on illustration board.
The display type was hand-lettered by the illustrator.
The text type was set in Nicholas Cochin by Thompson Type, San Diego, California.
Color separations by Bright Arts, Ltd., Singapore
Printed and bound by Tien Wah Press, Singapore
Production supervision by Stanley Redfern and Jane Van Gelder
Designed by Lisa Peters

Spelling was not regular in the days of Anne Bonney and Mary Reade.

In some reports Anne and Reade are spelled without *e*'s at the end.

Port Maria — 1720

THE AUTUMN SEAS are deep and dark
In Port Maria Bay;
The tunny fish all leap and sport
Around the bustling cay.

"What news, what news?" the people cry.
"What news bring you to town?"
"The governor has sent his ships
To pull the pirates down."

"The governor has sent his ships
With cannon all a-bristle,
And on the silver sea they sail
Just like a stinging thistle."

And silver the coins and silver the moon,
Silver the waves on the top of the sea,
When the pirate ship comes sailing in,
That gallant *Vanity*.

The Vanity

Now one small sloop that flew the black
Was Rackham's *Vanity*,
And it was manned by twelve brave lads
Upon the roiling sea.

When it was far and far from shore
Those twelve brave lads were ten,
For only on the sloop was known
That two of them weren't men.

Though only on the sloop was known
That one was bonny Anne,
And one was Mary Reade who dressed
Exactly like a man.

Anne Bonney   Mary Reade

"What news, what news?" the people cry.
"What news bring you to town?"
"Barnet has sailed his man-o'-war
To pull the pirates down."

"Barnet has sailed the *Albion*
Upon the autumn sea
To capture Rackham—'Calico Jack'—
And the gallant *Vanity*."

He slipped the western point of land,
All on that autumn day,
And there the pirates lay in wait
For their accustomed prey.

Barnet on board the Albion

The Albion

And silver the coins and silver the moon,
Silver the waves on the top of the sea,
When the pirate ship comes sailing in,
That gallant *Vanity*.

The autumn seas were deep and dark
Near Point Negril that day.
Two pirates stood upon the deck;
The rest, below, did play.

The rest, below, did drink and sport,
While up above the two
Kept silently their daily watch
For *Vanity* and crew.

"A ship, a ship!" did Mary cry.
And Anne cried, "Man-o'-war!"
But down below, Jack and his men
Did drink and sport some more.

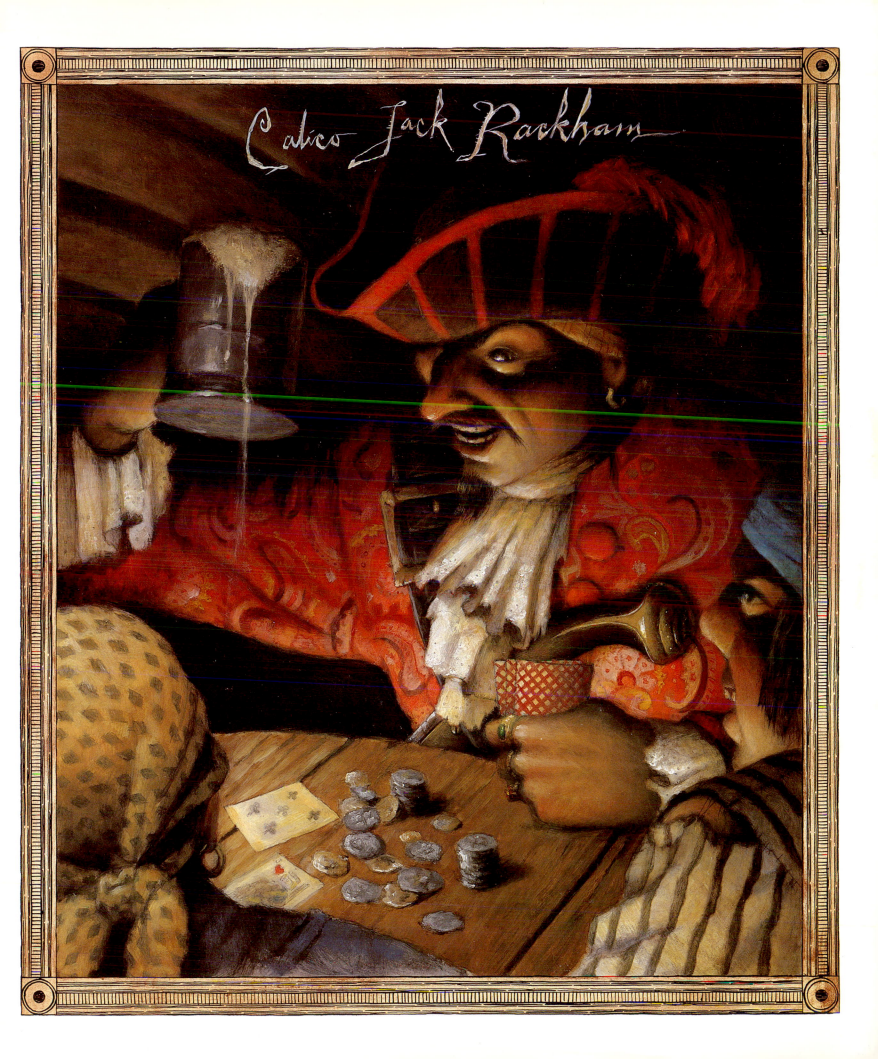

Calico Jack Rackham

The Albion engages the Vanity

And silver the coins and silver the moon,
Silver the waves on the top of the sea,
When the pirate ship comes sailing in,
That gallant *Vanity*.

"A ship, a ship!" did Mary cry.
"Come up and lend a hand."
But Rackham and his merry men
Came not to her command.

"A ship, a ship!" then Anne cried, too.
"Or else we will be taken."
But Rackham and his merry men
Their duties had forsaken.

So shoulder to shoulder and back to back,
Stood Mary and stood Anne;
Never was it said that they
Were feared of any man.

Defending the Varsity

Then one and two and through and through
Barnet's men plied their blades,
Until they'd overpowered both
Those doughty pirate maids.

Until Barnet had overcome
And brought them both to shore
Aboard the mighty *Albion*,
That bristly man-o'-war.

"What news, what news?" the people cry.
"What news bring you to town?"
"The *Vanity* is captured,
And two pirate queens brought down."

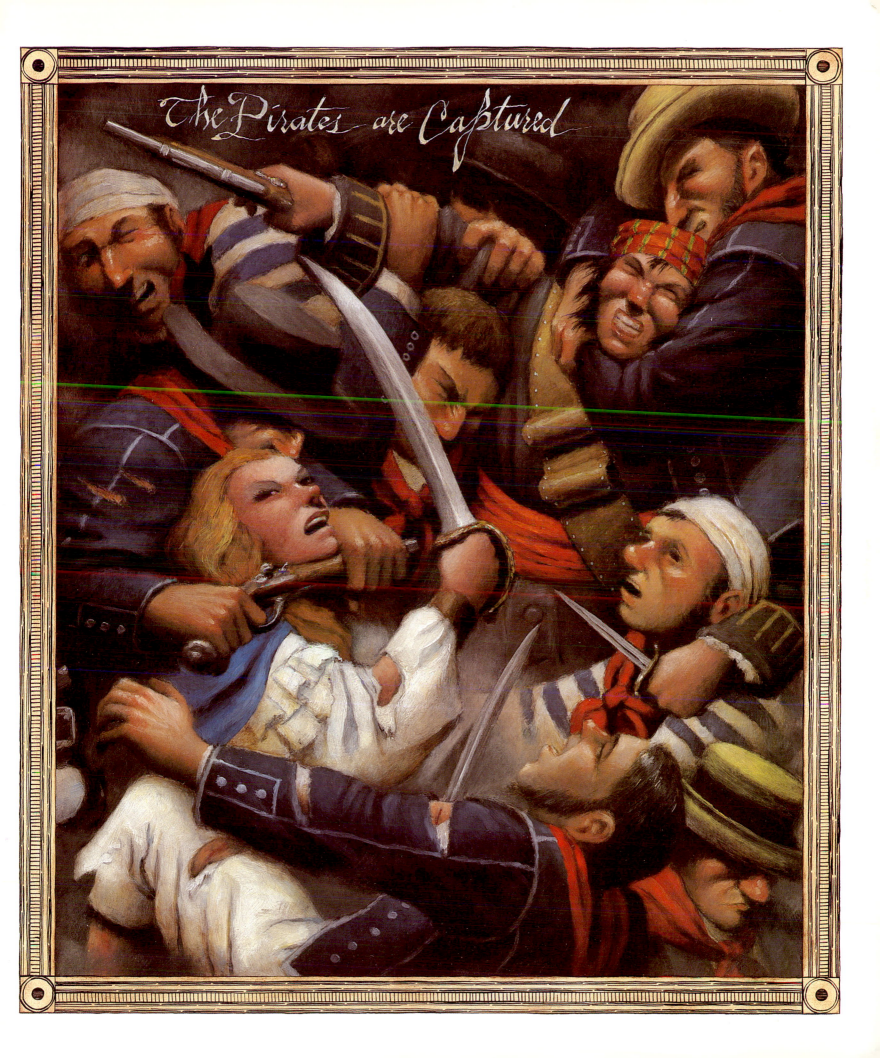

The Pirates are Captured

And silver the coins and silver the moon,
Silver the waves on the top of the sea,
When the pirate ship comes sailing in,
That gallant *Vanity*.

The Vanity Burns

The winter seas were dark and cold
Around Jamaica isle
When Anne Bonney and Mary Reade
Were readied for their trial.

They marched along the prison walk;
They passed Jack's cell block by.
Called Anne: "If you'd fought like a man,
My Jack, you'd need not die.

"If you had fought right by my side,
This day we'd both be free,
A-sailing in the open air
All on the silver sea."

The pirate queens before the judge
Each pleaded for her life.
"I am about to have a child;
I am a pirate's wife."

"Oh, you may be a pirate's wife,
Or by a man beguiled,
But never would I hang a maid
And kill the sinless child."

So Calico Jack and all his crew
Hanged on the gallows tree,
But bonny Anne and Mary Reade
Were by the judge set free.

Pleading their Bellies

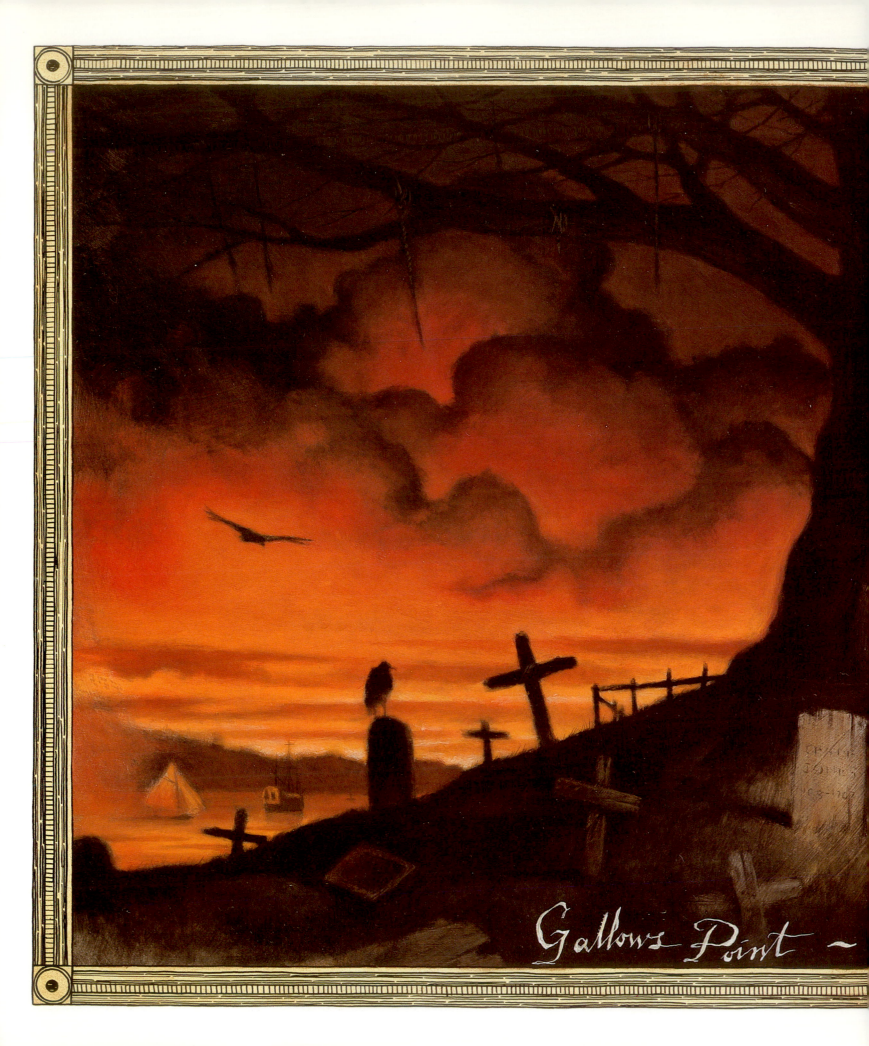

Gallows Point ~

And silver the coins and silver the moon,
Silver the waves on the top of the sea,
When the pirate ship comes sailing in,
That gallant *Vanity*.

Port Royal, Jamaica

And they say still on autumn nights
In Port Maria Bay,
Where tunny fish all leap and sport
Around the bustling cay,

A ghostly ship sails to and fro
Above the silver waves.
Then Jack and all his coward crew
Rise anxious from their graves

To sail the endless ocean round.
No! Never a rest get they.
But Anne and Mary's children's children
Round their households play.

Granny Annie   Grandma Mary

The Ghost Ship Vanity

And silver the coins and silver the moon,
Silver the waves on the top of the sea,
When the ghostly ship comes sailing in,
That gallant *Vanity*.

Author's Note

Anne Bonney (or Bonny) and **Mary Reade** were women pirates who sailed with "Calico Jack" Rackham's crew in the sloop *Vanity* along the coasts of America in the 1700s. In fact, they were the most famous women pirates in the world. Stories about their trial on November 20, 1720, filled the penny papers and news sheets of the day.

Captain Jonathan Barnet's man-of-war *Albion* captured the *Vanity* because only Anne and Mary were up on deck and willing to fight. The men were below, drinking rum and playing cards with nine turtle fishermen they had captured that day.

Anne visited her husband, Rackham, in prison and said to him: "I am sorry to see you there, but if you had fought like a man, you need not be hanged like a dog." Then she walked away.

She and Mary Reade "pleaded their bellies," meaning they were pregnant. Some say Mary died in prison and that Anne's father got her off free. She settled down as a poor but honest housewife with two children on a small Caribbean island. Others say Mary did not die but feigned death and was carried out of prison in a shroud. Still others, that both Anne and Mary were set free by the judge, then moved to Louisiana, where they raised their children and were friends to the end of their lives.

We can only imagine the stories they must have told at bedtime.